GUS & GERTIE
AND
THE MISSING PEARL

by JOAN LOWERY NIXON

pictures by DIANE DEGROAT

SeaStar Books

New York

Text © 2000 by Joan Lowery Nixon
Illustrations © 2000 by Diane deGroat

First published in the United States by SeaStar Books,
a division of North-South Books, Inc., New York.
Published simultaneously in Canada, Australia,
and New Zealand by North-South Books, an imprint of
Nord-Süd Verlag AG, Gossau Zurich, Switzerland.
Library of Congress Cataloging-in-Publication Data is available.
The art for this book was prepared using watercolor.
The text for this book is set in 16-point Nueva MM.

ISBN 1-58717-022-1 (trade binding)
1 3 5 7 9 10 8 6 4 2 TB
ISBN 1-58717-023-X (library binding)
1 3 5 7 9 10 8 6 4 2 LB

Printed by Proost N.V. in Belgium

For more information about our books, and the authors and artists who create them,
visit our web site: www.northsouth.com

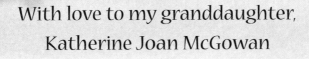

With love to my granddaughter,
Katherine Joan McGowan

—J. L. N.

CHAPTER 1

 Gertie and Gus hopped off the ferryboat onto the dock of Holiday Island and put down their suitcases. They were a fine-looking pair, dressed in their best vacation clothes.

But Gus's penguin flippers twitched nervously. The dock was deserted.

At the head of the dock, a taxi was parked, but no driver was in sight.

To the left of the dock was a rotting warehouse.

To the right of the dock was a battered building with a broken sign that read:

Under the sign was another sign:

From the OTEL came thumps and bumps, growls and yowls, and slam-bang music from the rackety keys of a tinny piano.

"The ferryboat captain told us to watch out for the Bad Guys," Gus said. "If Bad Guys are around, Gertie, then I don't think you should wear your beautiful, valuable deep-sea pearl."

"Nonsense. My pearl will be exactly the right thing to wear at the elegant Hotel de View," Gertie said.

"How do you know?" Gus asked. "We've never been to an elegant hotel like that."

"Relax, Gus," Gertie said. "Nothing bad is

going to happen. It's a lovely day to begin our vacation."

Gus glanced at the sky. "Only if you like rain," he said.

Gertie lifted her beak. "Just smell that wonderful sea air!" she said, taking a deep breath.

"We can smell sea air at home," Gus said.

"Just look at that beautiful ocean view!"

"We have an ocean view at home," Gus said.

"Take lots and lots of pictures," Gertie told him. "While we're on vacation, take pictures of everything!"

Gus sighed. He pulled out his Polaroid camera. He took a picture of the warehouse and a picture of the OTEL. He showed the pictures to Gertie.

Gertie frowned at the photos. "Especially, take pictures of *me*," she said.

Suddenly, the door of the OTEL burst open, and a wretched wharf rat sailed out.

Gus took a picture of him before the wharf rat picked himself up and charged back inside the OTEL.

"I'm glad we're not staying in *that* OTEL!" Gus said.

Just then, a voice above shouted, "Watch out below! Express mail coming through!"

Gus and Gertie ducked as a large pelican

sailed over their heads and bumped—*ker-thump, ker-splat!*—onto the dock.

The pelican staggered to his feet and picked up a handful of letters that had gone flying. "Good day for ducks," he said, "but not for pelicans. Either of you expecting any express mail?"

"No," Gus said as he tucked the photos he'd taken into his pockets. "We're waiting for the taxi driver to show up so he can drive us to the Hotel de View."

"I'm headed for the Hotel de View myself," the pelican told them. "I'll tell them to expect you."

He lowered his voice and nodded toward the OTEL. "This wharf isn't the place for nice folks like you. Just between you and me, watch out for the Bad Guys around here. And don't trust anyone but the taxi driver."

"Where *is* the taxi driver?" Gertie asked.

"Probably asleep," the pelican answered. "But don't worry. He'll show up—sooner or later."

The pelican stumbled into a flapping, lopsided run that carried him down the dock and into the air. "Happy vacation!" he shouted.

CHAPTER 2

A drop of rain splashed on Gus's nose. Another fell, then another.

"Oh, drat!" Gertie cried. "This rain will ruin my beautiful clothes!" She scurried as fast as she could into the nearest building—the old OTEL.

Gus picked up the suitcases and waddled along after her—right into the middle of the scummiest swarm of seagoing scallywags he had ever seen.

A pair of pirates whacked and smacked each other as they fought over a small treasure chest. An agile alligator, wearing fancy cowboy boots, scurried out of their way.

Rascally rowdies, wretched wharf rats, riffraff, and ruffians shouted and argued, pushed and shoved, and created a horrible hullabaloo.

"Uh-oh," Gus mumbled. "These must be the Bad Guys."

"Show them we're friendly," Gertie whispered. "Take their pictures."

Gus took lots of pictures. He spread them out so everyone could have a good look.

But suddenly, a huge, mean-looking desk clerk loomed over Gus and Gertie. He cleared his throat with a loud growl, then bellowed over the din, "Do you want to rent a room?"

"No, thank you," Gus yelled. "We came inside just to get out of the rain."

Gertie shouted, "The noise in here is terrible! What kind of state are these people in?"

The agile alligator shrugged. "What state? Me, I'm from the state of Louisiana," he said. "Just got here yesterday."

One of the pirates stopped smacking the other. "We're not from the States. We're a long way from home."

"Home?" A wharf rat wiped a tear from his eyes. "Blimey, it's been a long, long time since I've been home."

The piano player began playing "Home on the Range," but the desk clerk ignored him. Looking at Gertie, he snarled, "That's a mighty beautiful, valuable deep-sea pearl you've got there."

The piano player stopped playing. The swarm of scummy seagoing scallywags stopped what they'd been doing. Everyone turned to look at Gertie's beautiful, valuable deep-sea pearl. The room became so silent that Gus could hear the rain drumming on the roof.

"Blimey!" a rascally rowdy muttered. "Look at the size of that pearl!"

"Ought to fetch a pretty penny," a wretched wharf rat whispered.

"Uh-oh," Gus mumbled to himself. They should never have come inside the OTEL. His heart began to thump loudly as he wondered what would happen next.

CHAPTER 3

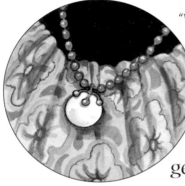

"Why don't you give your pearl to me?" the desk clerk said to Gertie. "I'll put it in the hotel safe, where no one can get to it."

Gertie looked nervously toward Gus. She didn't answer.

The wily weasel crawled out from inside the piano. "He's talking to *you*," he said to Gertie.

The desk clerk picked up the wily weasel and threw him out the door. But as soon as the desk clerk had turned around, the weasel sneaked back inside the room and into his hiding place inside the piano.

Gus didn't like anything about this OTEL. "May we please borrow an umbrella?" he asked the desk clerk. "I think Gertie and I had better wait outside."

One of the pirates stepped forward and bowed. "Don't go," he said to Gertie. "The members of the Bad Guys Club would like to give you a proper island welcome."

"A proper island welcome? That's a laugh!" the wily weasel shouted.

The lid of the piano fell down with a bang, and the weasel disappeared.

"What's a proper island welcome?" Gus asked. He wished that he and Gertie could leave this place. He didn't like the looks of the pirates' swords.

"We'll have a party in your honor," the pirate said. "And we'll dance island dances to entertain you."

"We'd better stay," Gertie whispered to Gus. "We can't be rude."

Before Gus could answer, the piano player banged out a clankity tune on the piano, and everyone in sight began to hop and jump and whirl and leap around Gus and Gertie.

Overhead, someone swung past on the chandelier, and the horrible hullabaloo grew so loud that Gus couldn't tell what was going on.

"Do something, Gus!" Gertie shouted.

Do what? Gus wondered. He wasn't a very good dancer, and someone was already playing the piano. There was only one thing Gus could do. He took lots of photographs of the Bad Guys doing their island dances, until his pockets were stuffed with instant photos.

Suddenly, up rushed the agile alligator, a yellow taxi driver's cap on his head. He tugged at Gertie's arm, trying to pull her out of the noisy mob.

"Y'all come with me," the alligator shouted. "I'll take you to your hotel."

"At last!" Gus said. "Why didn't you tell us you were the taxi driver?"

But Gertie began to scream, "Help! Help! Help! My beautiful, valuable deep-sea pearl! It's gone!"

Gus was so upset, he took a picture of Gertie screaming. He took a picture of the taxi driver. He even took a picture of himself taking a picture.

CHAPTER 4

The door to the OTEL crashed open. Filling the doorway was a large, imposing motorcycle officer.

"STOP!" he ordered.

Everyone stopped immediately. The room was silent.

"Who screamed?" the officer asked.

"Not us," said one of the pirates.

"Not us," piped up one of the wretched wharf rats.

"It must have been nobody," chimed in one of the rascally rowdies.

"That's right," agreed the ruffians and riffraff.

The wily weasel poked his head out of the top of the piano and pointed at Gertie. "It was her," he said.

"Yes, Officer. I'm the one who screamed," Gertie said. "Someone stole my beautiful, valuable deep-sea pearl!"

The officer looked slowly at everyone in the room. "Speak up," he said. "Who stole the lady's pearl?"

"Not us," said the pirates.

"Not us," said the wretched wharf rats.

"Not us," said the rascally rowdies.

"Not us," said the ruffians and riffraff.

"They're not telling the truth!" Gertie insisted. "One of them has stolen my beautiful, valuable deep-sea pearl!"

Gus came forward. He held out a fistful of photographs. "Officer," he said, "I took lots of pictures while the Bad Guys were giving us their proper island welcome. Take a look at these. They may give us the answer."

Gus spread out the photographs. Gertie and Gus and the motorcycle policeman studied them. Everyone else crowded around to look.

"These pictures show that every single one of you was involved in the theft," the officer said. "You're all going to jail."

"That's right! That's right!" the wily weasel cried. "They *all* did it!" He scampered out the door before the desk clerk could catch him.

"We took the pearl, but then someone stole it away from us," one of the pirates whined.

"It was us," one of the wretched wharf rats whimpered. "But we had it less than a minute when someone took it out of our hands."

"A whole minute? No fair!" one of the rascally rowdies complained. "We had it only a second."

"A whole second? We had the pearl for just an instant," the riffraff and ruffians muttered, "but we don't know where it went next."

"Oh, oh, oh! Where is my beautiful, valuable deep-sea pearl?" Gertie wailed.

"Don't worry, ma'am. We'll find your pearl," the officer told her. "We'll question the suspects at headquarters."

Gus took another look at the photographs. "I don't think you'll have to do that," he said.

The agile alligator picked up Gus and Gertie's suitcases. "Let's go, sir," he said.

"Wait," Gus told him. Gus said to the officer, "Take another look at these pictures. You'll see two clues that tell us who has Gertie's pearl."

The officer looked puzzled. "Two clues?" he asked. "What are they?"

CHAPTER 5

Gus bellowed at the top of his lungs, "Taxi!"

Off at the side of the room, a turtle woke up, stumbled to his feet, and said, "Yes, sir? Are you going to the Hotel de View?"

"This is the *real* taxi driver," Gus said. "You can see him wearing the yellow cap in this picture. It's one of the first I took when we came into the OTEL. And see this picture of a cowboy boot with a bulge in it? What would make a bulge that big?"

"My pearl!" Gertie shouted.

"Look again at the photographs," Gus said. "Can you find who stole the cap? Can you match the boot to the one who is wearing it?"

"I can!" Gertie said. "Where's that agile alligator? Arrest him, Officer!"

But the agile alligator had disappeared.

Gus and Gertie waddled out the front door of the OTEL after the officer.

"He's escaping in the taxi!" Gertie cried. "Look! He's driving up the hill."

"Hop in," the motorcycle officer told Gus and Gertie. "He may not know that road dead-ends at the Hotel de View. We'll catch him."

With a *ker-thump, ker-splat!* Gus and Gertie dived into the sidecar of the officer's motorcycle.

The wily weasel jumped in, too, along with the wharf rats and rascally rowdies.

Since there was no more room, the rest of the Bad Guys raced after them.

"Come on, matey!" a pirate shouted. "We stole the pearl first! It was rightfully ours! We'll get our revenge!"

"So will we!" one of the riffraff yelled. "That agile alligator is giving our club a bad name."

"Ha!" the wily weasel said. "He wasn't even a member."

The officer drove as fast as he could up the hill after the thief.

"Faster!" Gertie cried. "Make the motor-cycle go faster."

"It's carrying a lot of weight, so it's going as fast as it can," the officer answered.

"We'll take care of that," Gertie said. She threw out the wily weasel, the wharf rats, and the rascally rowdies. "Now, go faster!" she shouted.

Away sped the motorcycle on the road, faster and faster, with all the scummy scallywags running to keep up.

Gus pointed at the taxi ahead. "We're gaining on him!" he yelled.

The road wound up, up, up, until it reached the driveway of the elegant Hotel de View. The motorcycle screeched up behind the parked taxi. The pirates, rascally rowdies, wretched wharf rats, riffraff, and ruffians stumbled and scrambled and swarmed over the taxi.

But the agile alligator quickly jumped from the taxi and ran into the hotel.

"There he goes! Catch him!" Gertie screamed. They all ran into the hotel.

The thief was fast. The motorcycle officer was fast. All the members of the Bad Guys Club were fast. And Gus and Gertie were fast, too. With gigantic leaps and bounds, the entire group landed *SPLAT!* on top of the agile alligator, knocking him flat.

CHAPTER 6

Some of the hotel guests shrieked. The hotel manager looked faint. "I say! This was not in today's schedule!" he complained. "Who is responsible for this upsetting behavior?"

Gertie didn't answer. She just tugged her beautiful, valuable deep-sea pearl from the thief's boot. Gus hung the pearl around her neck.

The motorcycle policeman gripped the agile alligator's neck. "Come with me. I'll read you your rights," he said gruffly.

"Not until I tell him what a low-down, sneaky varmint he is," Gertie said.

The agile alligator sneered. "Go ahead and call me names," he said. "I don't care. I've got a thick hide."

"Hide?" one of the pirates said. "Why? Who's coming after us?" The whole swarm of seagoing scallywags looked nervous.

"There's no need for any of you to hide," Gertie said. She watched the officer take the agile alligator away. Then she beamed at the members of the Bad Guys Club.

"I would like to reward my friends with a plate of chocolate cookies and nut crunchies," she told the manager.

The wily weasel, wearing a hotel uniform, appeared with a tea tray. "And how about a nice cup of tea to go with the cookies?" he asked.

"Lovely idea. Maybe with a slice of lemon," one of the pirates said.

"With sugar and cream," one of the wretched wharf rats said.

Gertie turned to the guests of the Hotel de View. "Won't you all join us for tea and chocolate cookies?" she asked with a smile.

No one smiled back. Everyone stared in shock.

"Nut crunchies, then?" Gertie asked.

Some of the guests turned up their noses and sniffed. The hotel manager wrinkled *his* nose as though he smelled a dead fish.

"Will that be all, sir?" he asked Gus.

"No," Gus said. "My wife and I have a reservation for a vacation week at your hotel."

Gertie looked at all the unfriendly faces and spoke up. "Thank you, but we won't be staying," she politely told the hotel manager. "We have fresh sea air at home. We have a lovely ocean view at home. I think we'll be much happier at home than we would be here."

And they were.